Basketball Buddies

by Jean Marzollo and Dan Marzollo

Illustrated by True Kelley

Hello Reader! — Level 3

SCHOLASTIC INC.

Cartwheel
·B·O·O·K·S·®

New York   Toronto   London   Auckland   Sydney

Paul shot the ball at the basket. *Bang!*
It hit the rim.

Paul shot again. The ball flew over the
backboard.

Someone shouted, "Too Tall Paul!"

Paul hated that nickname. Paul's team-mate Brady stole the ball. He threw it to Paul. Paul began to dribble.

"LOOK OUT!" yelled Coach Reed.

But it was too late. Paul knocked two players over.

The whistle blew.

"Foul!" said the ref.

Coach Reed told Paul to sit down.

Paul felt awful. He thought being tall should make him a good player. But he wasn't good. He couldn't dribble well. And he bumped into people.

Paul really was too tall.

Finally, the game was over. Paul's team, the Lions, had won. No thanks to Paul.

"Good game," said Coach to the team. "See you at practice on Tuesday."

Paul started to leave with Brady.

"Paul," said Coach. "Can you come fifteen minutes early for extra practice?"

"Okay," said Paul. But he didn't want to.

When he got home, Paul ran up the stairs to his room.

He took out his collection of little action figures. He had little superheroes, little soldiers, and little spacemen.

He had good guys and bad guys. He set them up in fake wars. The good guys always won.

"Paul," yelled his mother. "Brady's here."

Brady was his best friend. He liked to play with action figures, too.

They started to play. While they played, they talked about basketball.

"Coach says I need more practice," said Paul. "He thinks I stink."

"Well, then, let's practice," said Brady.

They went outside to shoot baskets.
Brady was short. He liked to pass.
Brady passed and Paul made baskets.
"Playing with you is easy," said Paul.
"There aren't so many people. I don't bump into anybody."
"You need to practice with more people around you," said Brady.

That night Paul curled up in his bed. He made a wish that he wouldn't grow any more. He fell asleep and dreamed that he had shrunk. He was the same size as Brady!

When Paul woke up, he measured himself. He hadn't shrunk at all!

As he stepped up to the bus, Paul tripped. "Too Tall Paul has too big feet!" sang Maria. She was one of his friends. Did she mean to hurt his feelings? Paul didn't know. So he smiled. He pretended he didn't care. But he did.

By lunch Paul was hungry. He looked around the cafeteria. There were kids everywhere.

Across the room he saw Brady. Brady was sitting with the other kids on the team.

When Paul walked over, the kids stopped talking.

"Hi," said Paul. He sat down.

No one said a word. Paul wondered if his friends had been talking about him.

"Everybody going to practice tonight?" asked Maria.

"I have to go early," said Paul.

"What for?" asked Maria.

"Coach says I need extra practice," said Paul.

"Really?" said Maria. She winked at Brady.

"What's going on?" asked Paul.

"You'll see tonight," said Maria. She winked at Brady again.

That night Paul walked into the gym. His whole team was there.

"What are you doing here?" he asked.

"We decided to come early, too," said Brady. "If you need to come early, we need to come early. That was our secret at lunch. We wanted to surprise you."

Coach Reed said, "I like your team spirit."

Paul smiled. His friends really were his friends. "Let's play ball!" he said.

"Okay," said Coach. "Here's what we're going to do. Paul, stand beneath the basket. Maria, you dribble to the basket and shoot."

Paul got into position. Coach Reed told him, "Keep your eyes on the ball. When Maria shoots, try to block her shot. But don't touch Maria. If you touch her, that's a foul."

"Got it," said Paul.

"One more thing," said Coach. "If she misses, grab the rebound."

Maria started to dribble. All of a sudden, she yelled, "Too Tall Paul!"

Why did she say that? Paul was surprised. He took his eyes off the ball.

Maria dribbled around Paul and shot. The ball went into the basket.

Coach Reed said, "Paul, stay between the player and the hoop. Keep your eyes on the ball. Forget about your nickname."

Brady was next.

"Too Tall Paul!" he yelled.

Paul paid no attention. He kept his position. He kept his eyes on the ball.

Brady got ready to shoot. Paul threw out his arms.

Smack! He hit Brady on the arm.

"Ow!" yelled Brady.

Coach Reed said, "Paul, that's a foul. ALL you can touch is the BALL. As we say in basketball, 'ALL BALL.' Now, Brady, try it again," yelled Coach.

"No way," said Brady.

"Hakeem?" asked Coach.

"Okay," said Hakeem. "Too Tall Paul!" Hakeem dribbled the ball and shot it.

Paul put his arms high in the air. *Bam!*
He blocked Hakeem's shot! He didn't foul
Hakeem!

"Great!" yelled Coach. "All ball!"

After that, Paul started having fun.
He blocked shots. He grabbed rebounds.
He even made a few baskets. Most
important, he made fewer fouls.

But it was only practice. What would
happen in a real game?

"Good work," said Coach. "Everybody
go home and get ready to beat the Owls
tomorrow! It's the last game of the season."

Paul went home in the same car with Brady and Maria.

"Good night, Too Tall Paul," said Maria. She laughed.

"Good night," said Paul. He laughed, too. His nickname didn't bother him any more.

That night Paul didn't play with his
action figures. He lay on his bed and
stretched out as long as he could.

He dreamed about the tallest basketball
players in the world. Maybe one day he
would be one of them.

The next day was the big game. The Owls had won all their games this year. They had Jed, Chris, and Dawn.

But the Lions had Paul. And he was the tallest.

The game began with a jump ball. The referee threw the ball up between Paul and Jed. Paul tipped the ball to Brady.

When Paul came down, he landed on Jed.
The whistle blew. "Foul!" said the ref.

"Too Tall Paul!" someone shouted.
"Don't let it bother you," said Brady. "Go
to the basket. Get in position."

Jed dribbled the ball. Paul ran to the basket and got in position.

Jed drove in and shot the ball.

Paul jumped up. He hit the ball. But he didn't hit Jed. *ALL BALL! Yes!*

Brady grabbed the loose ball. He took it down the court. He passed to Maria. She aimed and scored for the Lions. *Yes!*

Now the Owls had the ball. They passed and dribbled their way to their basket.

Chris took a shot. He missed. Paul jumped up. He got the rebound! He passed to Brady. Brady dribbled to mid-court. Then he lost the ball. Now the Owls had it again.

Paul ran back to the basket. As he ran, he was careful. He didn't run into anyone.

Dawn shot the ball. Paul reached up and blocked it. *Yes!*

Finally he was fitting in. Everyone else could run around and chase the ball. But not Paul. His role was to grab rebounds, block shots, and sometimes make a basket.

It was a good game. The Owls won 28 – 22, but the Lions were happy. They had played better than ever.

Trophies were handed out. Most of the trophies went to Jed, Chris, and Dawn.

But the last one didn't.

The Most Improved
Player Award went to Paul.
It was the first trophy he had ever won.
    Paul heard his teammates start to chant.
What were they saying? He listened.
                    TOO TALL PAUL!
                    TOO TALL PAUL!
    As he went up to get his trophy, Paul
smiled. He held his head up, and he walked
tall. Now he liked being Too Tall Paul.

That night Paul measured himself on the wall. He was taller than before. Paul drew a new line. Next to it, he wrote the date and drew a little trophy.

Then Paul set his action figures around his trophy and went to bed happily.